HOW TO
Raise
Mom & Dad

INSTRUCTIONS FROM SOMEONE WHO FIGURED IT OUT

Josh LERMAN   ILLUSTRATED BY Greg CLARKE

DUTTON CHILDREN'S BOOKS

HOW TO RAISE MOM & DAD

Lerman

For my sister, Nina, who showed me how to raise our parents, and to Olivia and Lucy, who are doing their best to raise me. —J.L.

For Greta and Julian who provided the templates for the two young antagonists . . . sorry, I meant to say protagonists. —G.C.

DUTTON CHILDREN'S BOOKS | A division of Penguin Young Readers Group

PUBLISHED BY THE PENGUIN GROUP | Penguin Group (USA) Inc., 375 Hudson Street, New York, New York 10014, U.S.A. ✳ Penguin Group (Canada), 90 Eglinton Avenue East, Suite 700, Toronto, Ontario M4P 2Y3, Canada (a division of Pearson Penguin Canada Inc.) ✳ Penguin Books Ltd, 80 Strand, London WC2R 0RL, England ✳ Penguin Ireland, 25 St Stephen's Green, Dublin 2, Ireland (a division of Penguin Books Ltd) ✳ Penguin Group (Australia), 250 Camberwell Road, Camberwell, Victoria 3124, Australia (a division of Pearson Australia Group Pty Ltd) ✳ Penguin Books India Pvt Ltd, 11 Community Centre, Panchsheel Park, New Delhi - 110 017, India ✳ Penguin Group (NZ), 67 Apollo Drive, Rosedale, North Shore 0632, New Zealand (a division of Pearson New Zealand Ltd) ✳ Penguin Books (South Africa) (Pty) Ltd, 24 Sturdee Avenue, Rosebank, Johannesburg 2196, South Africa ✳ Penguin Books Ltd, Registered Offices: 80 Strand, London WC2R 0RL, England

Library of Congress Cataloging-in-Publication Data
Lerman, Josh.
How to raise Mom and Dad (instructions from someone who figured it out) / by Josh Lerman;
illustrated by Greg Clarke. — 1st ed.
p. cm.
Summary: Advice on how to manipulate your parents in order to avoid eating vegetables, extend your bedtime, or get a puppy. ISBN 978-0-525-47870-6   [1. Parents—Fiction. 2. Humorous stories.]
I. Clarke, Greg, date, ill. II. Title.   PZ7.L5583Ho 2009   [E]—dc22   2008013886

Published in the United States by Dutton Children's Books, a division of Penguin Young Readers Group, 345 Hudson Street, New York, New York 10014 ✳ www.penguin.com/youngreaders

DESIGNED BY HEATHER WOOD WITH GREG CLARKE
Manufactured in China ✳ First Edition ✳ 10 9 8 7 6 5 4 3 2 1

[] Wake up Mom and Dad
[] Help them get dressed
[] Feed them breakfast
[] Teach them how to make your lunch
[] Ask for things
[] Exercise their brains
[] Exercise their bodies
[] Leave the green veggies for them
[] Ask for things
[] Keep them focused on their chores
[] Tell them when they skip parts of a story
[] Tire them out so they'll get a good night's rest
[] Ask for things again

Now that you're older,

you're ready to help me with Mom and Dad. They mean well, but sometimes they need a hand.

Be sure to wake up Mom and Dad before it's light so they'll have plenty of time to stop feeling sleepy before they go to work.

But don't go to them—it's much nicer to shout really loud from your room until they get up and come to you, because exercise is healthy for grown-ups and it will help wake them up.

This is totally true.

Sometimes they take too long, and we
have to go and wake them ourselves.

Mom always tries to make the bed.
Which doesn't make sense, because
it's just going to get messed up later.
You can point this out to her.

Then you have to help Mom and Dad get dressed. They usually wear really boring clothes, so choose stuff that's more fun.

It will help them feel better about themselves.

Next comes breakfast. Mom and Dad will probably be practically snoozing still, so they need some good energy foods, which is anything with lots of sugar.

Now that you're in preschool, you'll have to
teach them how to make your lunch. Some things
that are okay for home—like carrots or yogurt—
are embarrassing at school. If you gradually stop
eating what they give you (bring it back home in
your lunch box) you can work your way to chips,
cookies, and pudding every day, like me.

In the car on the way to school is a good time to
ask for things, because that's where Mom and Dad
don't have anything else distracting them. Besides,
when you ask them for things, it makes them feel
like they're the bosses. You'll probably have to ask
again and again so they hear you over the radio.
Today we're going to ask for a puppy.

When Mom says, "We'll see,"
it means almost the same as "Yes."
   If Dad says, "We'll see," it means
he's gonna check with Mom.
   When Dad says, "Absolutely not,"
it means almost the same as "Yes."

If either of them says plain old "No," it
means "Maybe," so keep taking turns asking
each of them until it turns into "Yes."

After school, it's healthy to do something active. We can help Mom and Dad redecorate the living room and get exercise at the same time.

There will always be homework to do, but if you sign up to do the hardest, most complicated projects, Mom and Dad will do a lot of the work, which is good for their brains. This is a secret.

After we finish our homework, we can play before dinner.
Mom always likes to say, "How about a nice board game?"
I think they're called that because if you play them, you'll
be bored.

Instead, get piggyback rides from Dad. This will help his back and knees get stronger. He's always saying they're sore.

Dinner can get complicated, so really pay attention. For Mom and Dad to stay healthy they need to eat lots of green vegetables, but they're always trying to eat *less* of them by giving *more* to us. So, if you really care about Mom and Dad, eat as few green veggies as possible so there will be more for them.

What works best to avoid things like broccoli and green beans

and salad is distraction. That's why I move around and ask about dessert a lot. Or if they ask how your day was, don't tell them—that way they'll keep asking and forget about the vegetable thing. We could also ask them again about the puppy.

You'll eventually have to eat something green, but never give in on spinach, because that's the healthiest for them.

During bath time, you can help Mom and Dad keep the tub clean by sloshing the water around while you're playing.

You can also wash the floor by not using a towel when you get out. This means less laundry for them to do, too.

Cleaning our room is kind of like doing homework. You have to watch Mom and Dad carefully to make sure they don't get distracted from this chore.

Mom and Dad seem like good readers, but sometimes they mess up and skip parts when they read out loud. Listen hard and always tell them when they skip. Otherwise they might realize later on and feel really bad about it.

But even if you miss a skip, it doesn't matter, because you still get to snuggle.

There are a lot of things to remember at bedtime. Since the more tired you are, the better you'll sleep, it's a good idea to stay up as late as possible.

Also, it's our job to tire out Mom and Dad so they'll get a good night's rest, too.

First, ask for a glass of water, even if you're not that thirsty or you could get it yourself.

Next, come out of your room and say you're
itchy. You'll have to take a super-long time
showing them where, because sometimes the
itchy spot can move or totally new ones can
start right there on the spot. And you'll need
lotion rubbed on.

Then, because you were gone so long with the itchies, they'll have to kiss all your stuffed animals good night. Again.

When you've done everything else you can think of, tell them you're having bad dreams. Dad will always sing to make your bad dreams go away, which is good because he has a better voice than Mom. This is totally true. While Dad's singing, Mom should check the closet for monsters.

Once they're tired and can pay total attention, it's a good time to ask about the puppy again.

It's a lot of work to raise Mom and Dad, but in the end it's worth it. This is totally true.